I0648607

Wilhelmine E. Lichtenau

The Confessions of the Celebrated Countess of Lichtenau

Wilhelmine E. Lichtenau

The Confessions of the Celebrated Countess of Lichtenau

ISBN/EAN: 9783337847524

Printed in Europe, USA, Canada, Australia, Japan

Cover: Foto ©Raphael Reischuk / pixelio.de

More available books at **www.hansebooks.com**

MINNA ENCKEN,
Countess of Lichtenau?

THE

CONFESSIONS

OF THE CELEBRATED

COUNTESS OF LICHTENAU,

LATE MRS. RIETZ,

NOW CONFINED IN THE FORTRESS OF GLOGLAU AS A
STATE-PRISONER.

DRAWN FROM ORIGINAL PAPERS,

TRANSLATED FROM THE GERMAN.

WITH AN

Engraved Portrait of the Countefs,

AFTER AN

ORIGINAL PAINTING in the Poffeffion of the
COUNTESS MATUSKA.

———————

London:

PRINTED BY J. W. MYERS,

FOR W. WEST, NO. 27, PATERNOSTER-ROW.

1799.

TO

Mr. L——S H——Y, at Bath.

DEAR SIR,

I AVAIL myſelf of the departure of an Engliſh gentleman, who intends to ſet out for your city in a few days, to tranſmit you the tranſlation of a pamphlet which has lately appeared in German, and which is read with great avidity: If the peruſal of it ſhould afford you any amuſement, it will amply repay the few moments that I devoted to friendſhip.

It confiſts chiefly of the confeſſions of a woman, whoſe beauty firſt uſhered her into notice, and whoſe intrigues enabled her to maintain the conqueſts which her perſonal charms had made, even when viſibly on the decline. Had ſhe confined herſelf to the private circles of her amours, we might have heard little more of her than other modern

Thaïfes, but her ambition extended to politics, and the fatal effect of her influence in that line has ben felt, I am afraid, by more nations than one in the prefent unhappy conteft with the demagogues of France.

The original papers which were found in the poffeffion of the Countefs when fhe was arrefted, and from which thefe confeffions have been drawn, were communicated to the Author of this pamphlet by a Member of the Committee appointed to enquire into the tranfactions of this intriguing woman. The language, however, was fo grofs and indelicate, that, out of refpect to religion and morality, it was neceffary to omit them. It was alfo thought proper to omit many political paffages, and wait till a proper opportunity prefented itfelf to bring them to light. Then you will be furprifed to find the part this infamous woman and her creatures acted in many of the fcenes which have lately been exhibited in Europe. There never was a perfon, perhaps, whofe fall has been lefs lamented by all parties. She was, as fhe ftates herfelf in her confeffions, the daughter of a trumpeter; fhe lived, for fome time, as a maid fervant with her eldeft fifter, who was early initiated into all the myfteries of Venus; but the fifter treated her fo ill, that fhe was obliged to return to her mother's, where fhe was firft noticed by a young man of the *higheſt* rank. At this period ſhe was about fifteen years of age. Her proteſtor ordered lodgings to be provided for her, and proper maſters to inſtruſt her in reading and writing; and, as ſhe was of a very apt difpofition, he taught her French himſelf, and was highly gratified with the progrefs of his pupil in other polite accompliſhments, ſuch as dancing, drawing, &c. Such was her afcendancy over the heart of her benefaſtor, that he brought her to Potfdam, where ſhe lived in a ſtile that could not efcape the penetrating eye of the old K--g, ſo that, in order to avoid any difagreeable confequences on that head, it was thought ad. vifeable that ſhe ſhould travel, and that in as private a manner as poffible. She met with many accidents in her way to Paris, particularly in pafling through Champagne, where her carriage was broken, · which endangered her life. Her royal lover, in 1792, wrote to her that he had taken poffeffion of the ſcene of her misfortune.

To make amends for the privacy in which ſhe had travelled, ſhe ſhone forth, all at once, in Paris, as a ſtar of the firſt magnitude, in the faſhionable hemifphere; her *petit foupirs* were numerouſly attended by the gay, the giddy, and the vain. Veſtris taught her to fail through all the mazes of harmony, but, after all, the want of an early education was vifible in her manners and language. Her principal tafte lay in drefs, for almoft every moment that fhe could fpare from amufement was devoted to her toilet.

The attentions paid to her in Paris, by perfons of the firft rank, inflated her vanity to fuch an ex-cefs, that fhe was impatient to revifit her native country in order to relate all the fine compliments which had been paid to her in her abfence, but this vanity was not a little mortified when fhe was obliged, or rather condemned, to marry Mr. Rietz, a chamberlain of the Prince, who had been raifed to that rank from the low ftation of a gar-dener. The thoughts of being obliged to give her hand to a man devoid of education, who could only boaft of poor, but honeft, parents, preyed fo inceffantly on her fpirits, that fhe, at length, obtained a divorce from him, though fhe had born him feveral children. Though her per-fonal charms could no longer maintain their full empire over the heart of her protector, yet fuch were the refources of her arts, that, notwithftand-ing he was gradually eftranged from her couch, yet he conftantly vifited her drawing-room. His protection, however, was not confined to her alone; it extended to all her family. Mirabeau, in his Secret Hiftory of the Court of Berlin, thus fpeaks of the marriage of her fifter:——" On Sunday, (the 12th, 1786) at the principal inn in Berlin, the marriage of the Countess Matufka and a Pruffian officer, named Stutherm, was celebrated. The Countefs is a fifter of Mademoifelle Henke (Madam Rietz;) fhe thought to have married a Polifh gentleman, who, fome months fince, withdrew. Once deceived, fhe next made choice of a young officer. The K--g has given money, and money enough. It is fuppofed that Madam Henke, who now is faid not to be married to Rietz, will retire and live with her fifter, that fhe may not impede the projeᴄ̄s formed to enjoy the maid of honour in peace." The following paffages are alfo taken from the fame work:——" Mademoifelle Henke, or Madam Rietz, as you think proper to call her, has petitioned the King (December 23, 1786) te be pleafed to let her know what fhe is to expeᴄt, and to give her an eflate on which fhe may retire. The Sovereign offered her a country-houfe, a t the diftance of fome leagues from Potfdam. The lady fent a pofitive refufal, and the King, in return, will not hear of any mention made of an eftate. It is difficult to fay what fhall be the produᴄt of this confliᴄt betwixt cupidity and avarice."

" Madam Rietz, who, of all the miftreffes of the Sovereign, has moft effeᴄtually refifted the inconftancy of men, and the intrigues of the wardrobe, has modeftly demanded the Margravate of Schwedt from the King, to ferve as a place of retreat, and four gentlemen to travel with her fon, as with the fon of a monarch. This audacious requeft has not difpleafed the King, who had been offended by the demand made of an eftate. He, no doubt, has difcovered that he is highly refpefted, now that he receives propofitions fo honourable."

She vifited Italy foon after her divorce, where fhe diffipated fuch immenfe fums that fhe was obliged to return to repair the continual drain. Dear variety was now her motto. Her attachment to the young Count, Louis Bouillé, is thought to have tended very much to induce the Court of Berlin to join in the invafion of France. Pains were taken, after his difmiffal, to attach her to an Irifh nobleman, Lord T————n. Whatever may have been the fatal confequence of her influence, fhe may ferve as an example, that, however vice may flourifh for a while, its reign is of fhort duration. "The demife of her proteftor put an end to all her confequence," fays one of her biographers, "her revenues, her flatterers, and her liberty, and in a moment, annihilated the Juno of anti-jacobinifm." She is now imprifoned in the caftle of Glogau, execrated by the poor, whom fhe oppreffed, and detefted by the nobility, whom fhe endeavoured to rival in power and fplendor, and unpitied by all. Her *château* at Charlotten-

berg was lately fold to Mr. Eckhardt for an immenfe fum.

Thus I have given you a fhort fketch of the
life of this extraordinary woman. I hope to fee
you foon, and hear from your own lips what effect
her confeffions have made on you as a man, and
more particularly as an Englifhman.

I am, with true regard,

Your's truly,

RICHARD B—T—N.

Hamburgh, March 8, 1799.

MY CONFESSIONS.

I WAS born in a fmall village called Deffau, at the very time when the portentous comet, with its luminous tail, threatened the affrighted inhabitants of my native country with peftilence, famine, war, and all the attendant train of mifery. I mean in the year of our Lord one thoufand feven hundred and ———. Whoever is the leaft acquainted with the hiftory of that comet will not be at a lofs how to find out the remaining figures to complete the year of my birth. My father, Heaven have mercy upon his foul! was an honeft good kind of man, and obliged to maintain himfelf, his wife, my fifters, and me, with the produce of his earnings; his name was Encke; his profeffion that of a trumpeter. Our mode of living was fuch as behoved the family of a man in his humble line, and had not my mother, at intervals, found means to make a few perquifites, we might have fared ftill worfe.

B

But, dear woman! fhe was an induftrious being, and would contrive it fo as to enable my honeft father to fit down to a joint of meat, at leaft, twice or thrice a week. This my poor father liked very well, and would pay his dear partner many a well deferved compliment on the occafion.

My father had lately been called to Potfdam, to be one of his Royal Highnefs's band of mufic, in confequence of which we fixed our abode at Berlin. In the capital my mother continued her former trade, and had very good cuftom for herfelf, whilft at the fame time fhe would never neglect any occafion of clandeftinely making fome good bargain or other for my eldeft fifter and me, either with fome young wealthy debauchee, or an old married man ; thefe bargains produced watches, clothes, cafh, &c.

In this way of living, in a kind of ftyle, without much concern, my father was highly pleafed; yet, every now and then, he would—and Heaven knows why—fly into a violent fit of paffion, and, in thofe fits, would generally make ufe of a kind of manual argument to convince my good induftrious mother of her duty as a wife. The fourteenth anniverfary of my birth happened to fall on the twenty-ninth day of the month of February, Bif-fextile, when my father entered upon an argument of this impreffive nature, and his paffion rofe fo high that it killed him on the fpot.

My mother was now a widow, and we all prof-pered beyond our warmeft expeɛtation. Our fa-ther being gone, we immediately hoifted our co-lours publicly at Berlin, and why fhould we not, as our reputation was pretty well eftablifhed, and known all over the town? Our good mother's province was to hold out the lure to empty the purfes of unwary youth, and to pluck up by the root the very laft feather of the conceited fool; all this was performed on a methodical fyftem. Our houfe was a fort of rendezvous, where the Jew and the Chriftian could affemble without any interruption.

My eldeft fifter had the good fortune to ftrike the fancy of a Prince, and to be chofen by him for his miftrefs. It became my humble lot, at that time, to wait on her, which, however, did not hinder me from conduɛting my own little concerns in private, for they were well worth continuing. What bufinefs had I to toil and work, whilft my admirers could adminifter to my wants and wifhes! Ducats and fine clothes were my motto, and who-ever would furnifh me with thefe was fure to fuc-ceed. My fifter, one day, happened to be off her guard with her favourite, for, befides the Prince, she had an intrigue with a Silesian Count, of the name of Matufchka. She was just sitting on the sopha, in a careless posture, when, all of a sudden, the Prince entered the room. His eyes sparkled with indignation, and in the first fit of his anger he took my sister by the hair, pulled her off the sopha, and then knocked the glasses, china, &c. girandoles, chandeliers, and every article of furniture in the room, to pieces. The Count, with the aid of my mother, fled through the window, and might thank his saints for the narrow escape, for his life was at stake, and the Prince would have ran him through without hesitation.

He loaded my mother with all the reproaches his rage could suggest, called her a procurefs, &c. Poor woman! she was innocent, and, of course, the treatment affected her to the very quick. But at once she took me by the hand, and, stepping up to the Prince, thus addressed him : " Please your Royal Highness, I protest to Heaven, and all his Saints, that I am quite innocent. The Count is the girl's own choice. I am as innocent as the child unborn. Here, take my little Minna instead of her; she will keep true to you; she is susceptible of gratitude; I can pledge my word that you will find what I say to be true. Behold, and please your Royal Highness, behold this beau-

tiful innocent; behold this lucid eye, this harmo-
nious fhape, this flender waift, and then the rofe-
bud; her lively converfation will diffipate your
cares, when collected on your brow; and then fuch
fallies of wit, fuch fprightly fayings, fuch flafhes
of merriment, that time will dance away with down
on his feet in her company." The Prince fmiled
at this fublime piece of oratory, which my mother
had got by rote, like a parrot; forgot all that had
happened, and fince that very moment chofe me
for his favourite.

With this amiable Prince I lived in uninterrupted
happinefs, but his uncle, the fage, the politician, and
the hero, began to interfere with our little love-
concerns, and loudly inveighed againft his nephew's fathering feveral of my children, and the
people publicly calling me his miftrefs. It did
not become, he thought, the deftined ruler of a
great and powerful nation to be governed and
duped by women and a fet of idle parafites. Such
creatures, he faid, were generally connected with
a gang of adventurers, for whom no honeft man
could have the leaft efteem, becaufe they had no
other aim than to creep into favour, under the
protection of a proftitute, and, as foon as they had
obtained it, would interfere with the moft ferious
and momentous concerns of the ftate, betray whole

nations, exhauſt the very ſources of the common wealth, and commit aᵭs of violence and injuſtice. Such and the like nonſenſe would frequently flow from the old man's lips, and the Prince, who, in faᵭ, was ſomewhat overawed by his aged uncle, adviſed me to retire to my native town till the ſtorm was over, and the horizon cleared up again. In conſequence of his advice, I repaired to Deſ-ſau, accompanied by my mother, where I was ſoon afterwards delivered of a ſon. The Prince often came to viſit me in my retirement, and our meetings were crowned with unſpeakable bliſs.

To make the old man quite eaſy, and the better to enable ourſelves to carry on our mutual inter-courſe, the Prince propoſed a match between me and his favorite valet, Rietz. His uncle, he thought, would the ſooner forget me, and his foes, as well as mine, would, by this marriage, be brought to ſilence. I entered into the ſcheme, became Mrs. Rietz, and returned unconcerned to Berlin. To the old grumbler I was repreſented as an ignorant country wench, without any turn for intrigue, and incapable of governing the Prince, and ſtill leſs of involving him, even in the moſt diſtant manner, in any foreign concern. This completely quieted the old man, and I paſſed my time in the greateſt peace and tranquillity.

The long wifhed-for moment arrived at laft; the old fellow died, and my dear admirer afcended the throne. An extenfive field of action now opened before my eyes; " This is the time, faid I to myfelf, to form my fyftem; to govern, to rule, to enrich, my friends, and to humble the pride of my inveterate foes."

I am forry, and this I confefs with the moft heart-felt compunction, to have, through artifice and malice, robbed the K—g of the love of his people, for he really was a good man, and his humanity extended to all the creation. Oh! what a fource of happinefs this love proved to his feeling heart, and how often have I heard him exclaim, " Thank God, my people are happy, and fo am I through their happinefs!" This, however, was no more than a deception, for I, and thofe that were about him, never would give him an opportunity to caft a look into the moft interior recefles of the fyftem of government, and thus he was deceived, and actually thought that his fubjects were happy; but it was not his fault, it was mine, for his heart was benevolence itfelf.

The vile creatures who flocked to my train, through the moft infamous windings, attempted to deprive him of the love of his people, and became, in the fulleft extent of the word, his rulers. But I muft return to my own ftory.

I was now poffeffed of princely palaces, and the pomp of royalty was difplayed in all my apartments. Minifters, generals, princes, and noblemen, crowded my levees and courted my fmiles. What could be more natural than that the invidious fhould watch every ftep I took? The privilege of being thus noticed by a great prince could not fail to excite jealoufy, and an opportunity foon offered to lay the foundation of my ruin. The K—g, who was fond of variety in love, conceived a violent paffion for Mifs V——, a young lady of the Court, a lady endowed by nature with the moft exquifite charms fhe could beftow upon a favourite mortal. The name of Mifs V——, till this very hour, is never mentioned but with the higheft refpect. At the firft outfet her virtue withftood every attack; but, when the K—g became more preffing, and the nobility joined him in his purfuit, fhe yielded at laft, but on condition of a left-handed marriage. The K—g lived, during the fpace of one full year, in the greateft happinefs with Mifs V——, and I might, perhaps, have been entirely flighted and forgotten, had not a difh of chocolate, adminiftered at a proper time, rid me of a detefted rival, and the K—g of a love-fick enthufiaft. I now once more was the toaft, and the fovereign-arbitratrix of my Royal Lover's mind. Whatever did not fuit my plan, or harmonize with my views, was removed from the fight of the monarch, and none but thofe who were of my party had accefs to the clofet.

My hufband had likewife been put in the way of exercifing the power of influence, and of laying by treafures. Yet I was often vexed when I faw that certain men, who could not poffibly be denied, got admiffion to the K—g; for I was always afraid, left, fome time or other, they might have the affurance to paint me in my true colours.

It became advifeable, however, to think of fecuring a confiderable part of my wealth, for which purpofe I projected a journey to Italy, where I meant to difpofe of my property as advantageoufly as I could. As I lived in the firft ftyle of grandeur, the K—g was prevailed on to confer the title of Countefs of Lichtenau on me at the Court of Vienna. The requeft was granted, and to enable me to maintain the dignity and rank, I obtained a feparation from Mr. Rietz. From that very inftant I was, on my return from Italy, admitted to all the circles and the affemblies at Court. My daughter, who had been decorated with the title of Countefs of the Mark, was to marry none but a Count, and the King intended to beftow an adequate dowry on her. Her fuitors were many, and amongft the reft Count Stolberg was preferred.

As the K—g was fond of amufement, I was pleafed to fee that W—— and B—— entertained him with the Roficrucian nonfenfe, and other magic tricks. Thefe ventriloquifts could do me no harm; nay, on the contrary, they were the means of perfuading the K—g to any thing. It was at this very period that I filled all the offices of Court with wretches of my own choice. All the King did, fpoke, and undertook, was faithfully reported to me, and hence he muft inevitably remain entangled in my net.

The French war broke out, and then it might be faid I was truly launched into my own element. B—— was employed by the Cabinet of Vienna and the Court of St. —— to bring things to bear with our K— g, and he was feveral times obliged to undertake journeys to Vienna and to Italy. The coalition was agreed on, and we marched againft France. This war was the very thing I wanted; for, as the King was bufy, I took all the opportunities I could to make him fenfible of the licentioufnefs of the people; and, as the expences had increafed, and became more multiplied than before, I had fair play to accumulate treafure in proportion. My chief contributors, however, were Auftria and ——, for they would pay me abundantly for the part I took in perfuading the King not to recede from the coalition. But no man ever knew how to get me over to his interest better than P—. For this purpose, he employed his relation T————, who paid me his addresses for a long time, had apartments in my palace, and partook of my table and carriage. Money was my motto, just the same as it had been at the time when Jews and Christians reforted to the house of Minna Encke, in Spandau-street. It is a pity that this war, or, at least, the coalition, did not last a little longer, for then I might, in fact, have realized my favorite project, of purchasing some principality, for the flood of presents flowed in without intermission.

We returned home without having effected any thing, and my chief object was to secure the King's affections by all the variety of pleasure and entertainment I could possibly think of. I had in my palace a neat little theatre, where I entertained the King with such pieces as seemed to have been written for the very purpose of charming the fenfes. My actresses were chosen from among the handsomest girls in all Berlin. I always made them appear in such dresses as would add, if possible, to their charms. With the same view, I generally chose the subjects of the entertainment from mythology; for instance, Jove and Leda, Venus and Cupid, Hymen's Wake, &c. A celebrated man of learning of the capital, the manager of my little theatre, took with a smile the presents which the en-chanted monarch gave him, and since that time abstained from inveighing against the King's mistress in his satirical writings.

Some disturbances, which took place in the provinces, and particularly at Berlin, gave me the fairest opportunity to induce the King to prohibit the publication of all such works as treated of liberty, equality, and the imprescriptible rights of man, and in general of all such trash.

A kind of inquisition, which, through my interference, was introduced throughout the country, enabled me to obtain a knowledge of all the pamphlets that represented me in my true colours to the world, and to suppress them. And, if at any time some determined scribbler had the audacity to transgress the limits of the liberty of thinking and writing, it would, through the medium of my creatures, represent the act as an attempt nothing short of high treason against the King's Majesty itself, in which case imprisonment for life, or banishment from the King's dominions, was the unavoidable consequence. Such was the fate of the merchants Z———. C———, of Doctor K———, and of Captain L———.

Upon the whole, my emissaries and I had, at that time, the most absolute and unprecedented sway.

The fubject felt all the weight of my defpotic oppreffion, and the lafh of my fcourge. Frank-nefs in fcientific debate, cordiality in mutual communication, and hilarity in company, en-tirely difappeared. My fpies were dreaded every where. Upright magiftrates, who pro-nounced fentence according to the dictates of right and reafon, were difmiffed; thofe of the clergy, who ventured to preach common fenfe, loft their places, and were banifhed the country; the moft important trials were fuperfeded, becaufe the ver-dicts were expected to fall out againft me and my friends. Several of the public offices I caufed to be given to my creatures; I forged warrants of arreft, and orders of the cabinet; rewarded fpies, informers, and runners, with large fums of money and honourable offices; nay, I had, without any apparent reafon, a young lady arrefted, merely becaufe I dreaded that her beauty would fup-plant me. In a word, whatever did not pafs through my hands, or was not fubfervient to my fchemes, was fure to be crufhed. A certain man in office, who repeatedly had embezzled the public money, fued for my protection; I had him created a nobleman, and chief judge of the Criminal Court. But, in return for this good office, he was, from gratitude, bound to give his verdict in every caufe that concerned either me or my friends, as I would have it. He did indeed once attempt to recede from it, and to have it his own way, in the affair with Mifs Belderbufh; this was the name of the young lady, juft before mentioned; but I had influence enough to punifh him for his temerity; he was difmiffed, and banifhed the kingdom. This was likewife the lot of the Countefs D——, and the Privy Counfellor G——, againft whom a fufpicion of being concerned in a fcheme of poifoning was urged, and who were compelled to leave the P——— dominions. Such was at that time the power of the trumpeter's daughter, whofe favour, thirty years back, might be purchafed for a dollar.

Rietz, my late hufband, perfectly agreed with me in this point. This man, who from a common labouring gardener, had rifen to the office of a Privy Chamberlain, had made it his ftudy, and completely acquired, the art of bending and twifting his lord and mafter to whatever fhape and form I wifhed, and of imbuing him with the moft erroneous notions concerning his fubjects. He generally ufed to keep a pack of large maftiffs, that would frighten away every un-welcome fuppliant; and if ever any one had the audacity of attempting to approach the K—g, he was fure to be treated with a found caning, and a few blows in his face, and might think himfelf well off with the lofs of half a dozen of his teeth. As an inftance of this, a poor young fellow, the only fon of a fhoemaker, who had attempted to prefent a petition in behalf of his diftreffed parents, was, by Mr. Rietz himfelf, well threfhed, then fent to the watch-houfe, and, by way of a lafting remembrance of his temerity, forced as a foldier into a ftationary regiment. Of all this the King knew nothing, for his good and tender heart prompted him to do juftice and grant protection to the very meaneft of his fubjects; he verily believed that his people were all happy and content; and had he the leaft idea of any fuch cruel outrage, the perpetrator would have been punifhed in the fevereft manner, even had it been my darling Rietz himfelf. But his dogs were trained to know every avenue, fo that an accefs to the King was rendered altogether inacceffible. He alfo knew how to avail himfelf of the influence he had over the King, and by the proper management of this very influence a number of petitions and complaints were fuppreffed, and condemned to the flames and filence, many an order of the cabinet was deceitfully obtained, and the beft places under government were given to our party. This indeed was not the means to infpire the people with love for their Sovereign, but what was that to us? Provided the monarch could be made to believe that all were happy and fatisfied, and that there was no reafon for complaint, all was well enough; nay, the people themfelves facilitated our views, and ftrengthened the King in his good creed. On many public occasions, they would hail their prince with loud applause and acclamation. *God save the King* was sung in German at the theatres and concerts, and the best poets of the nation exhausted all their Parnassian fire to produce a good parody of this favourite popular song of the people of England. Every pamphlet, every newspaper, every production of the press, bore testimony to the happiness of the people; in every one of them the nation was represented as laying their allegiance and love at the foot of the throne, ready to spend their last shilling, and shed the last drop of their blood, in his support. Thus this easy good-natured prince was led to believe that every thing was right, and that he lived in the heart of his subjects, which he certainly did, notwithstanding our oppression and injustice.

It must be confessed, that good master Rietz carried his insolence rather too far. The wealth which, through just and unjust means, had flowed into his coffers had inflated him with pride and vanity; he became presumptive, brutal, and rough; he therefore thought he might bear down every thing before him by main force. The tricks, which he played behind his master's back, deprived the King of a share of the affections of his people; distress, fear, and smothered resentment, had got possession of every heart. Very often the blood of

the defperate wretch would flow from this fole con-
fideration, that nothing was to be done with the
K—g, let the caufe be ever fo juft. This indeed was
too hard. I have, however, pretty well fucceeded
in mortifying his prefumption. This proud *ci-
devant* gardener's boy once took it into his head to
fall in love with Madam B.———s. He had even
gone fo far as to projeft a marriage with her,
when at once a warrant was iffued from the cabinet,
by virtue of which the lady was removed from the
Berlin ftage, and an end was put to the farce.
His mind was tortured with mortification and
fhame, and he found himfelf reluftantly obliged to
fee his fair one, without friend or proteftor, caft on
the wide world. But the wretch deceived me
after all, and cringed and flattered till I winked at
his prefumption, and let him bear away his prize.

As the K—g evinced a great predileftion for
every thing fupernatural, a predileftion which he
had derived from his intercourfe with the Roficrufians, and from all the magic tricks they had played
off before him, I was highly pleafed at the arrival
of the Chevalier Pinetti de Mercy. This man
fought my proteftion, and I was very willing to
grant it. Furnifhed with numberlefs recommenda-
tions, and dreffed out, like a nobleman, with laced
and embroidered clothes, watches, and rings, fet
with valuable brilliants, his accefs to the king was

c

not very difficult. This fellow in fact was nothing
but a charletan, but he was well fkilled in the art
of deception, fo that I faw his mountebankifm
might be of ufe to me and my party. His tricks
with cards confifted in nothing but legerdemain,
and I placed no value on them; on the other
hand, his phyfical deceptions, as he pleafed to term
them, were the more entertaining. The K—g was
highly pleafed with his phyfical deceptions, made
him a prefent of five thoufand dollars for the
erection of a theatre, and gave him the title of
Profeffor of Phyfic of the Court, with a penfion of
fix hundred dollars a year. This prodigality of
courfe rouzed the envy of the philofophers of
Berlin, and, among others, one Profeffor Kofmann
ventured to publifh a treatife on Pinetti's work, in
which he called his paltry tricks the *ne plus ultra* of
natural philofophy. The Profeffor, in this pamphlet, endeavoured to prove, that every thing was
pretty clear and natural, and that the famous
Pinetti was neither more nor lefs than a common
legerdemain conjuror. The chevalier was very
much difpleafed at this publication, and wrote the
Profeffor word, that, if he did not immediately fup-
prefs his work, and apologize for the epithets of
conjuror and *mountebank*, he, Mr. Pinetti, would
give the Profeffor an anfwer *à l'Italiana*. Pinetti
was in right earneft, and preferred his complaints
againft Kofmann to the K—g. The Profeffor jufti-

fied himfelf by tranfmitting his to Majefty a copy of
the work, and affuring him, that his only motive
for writing it was to give a hint to the ftudents of
the military fchool not to fuffer themfelves to be
deceived by appearances. The K—g fmiled, and
Kofmann got off without any farther moleftation.
This work has neverthelefs done poor Pinetti a great
deal of injury. He wrote to me from St. Peterfburg: " Dear Countefs, It is enough to make a
man run crazy, to fee how my phyfical experi-
ments have been hiffed and hooted at Konigfberg;
on my firft performance, the greateft number of my
fpectators had the pamphlet of that meddling Profeffor Kofmann in their hands, and laughed and
fcoffed at me; and after the third exhibition I was
compelled to clofe my theatre, or exhibit to empty
benches.   Here the patriarch of Jacobinifm,
that infernal Kant, lives and plays his tricks;
here is the very den of the red-capped Jacobin
gang, and his Majefty would do well, for the bene-
fit of his own dominions, to deftroy this neft of
wafps and vipers, and to prohibit Kant, who befides
is an old man, all manner of reading and writing.
Ah! with what extacy all flocked at Berlin to the
divine Pinetti! the high and the low, the wealthy
and the great, were charmed, whenever Pinetti
deigned to addreffed them. Here in St. Peterfburg
things go on better, &c."

At this time I had made a fecond journey to Italy, and brought to Berlin the celebrated Vizano and her hufband. I could not poffibly have procured the K—g a greater pleafure than the opportunity of feeing and admiring thofe two famous dancers. As Vizano had left the ftage at Vienna on account of his being fo violently in love with her, I thought I could keep her at Berlin; but thefe capering wretches had no other view but to make money, and would on no account enter into my projects. I therefore had a number of pupils and figuranti regularly trained up, who alternately performed on my little private theatre, which anfwered my purpofes very well. To thefe means I then had recourfe; for, as I began to be aware that my charms were on the decline, and incapable of any longer rivetting the fetters of my lover; and, as he befides was fond of variety, I invented a thoufand novelties, and called forth all my ingenuity to retain him in my net.

To this point I fucceeded fo completely, that the K—g never undertook a ftep in his amours without confulting me. Befides, I had by that time acquired a perfect knowledge of the myfteries in which I had been initiated during my ftay in France and Italy, and for which I had paid very confiderable fums. This confifted in the mixture of certain narcotic ingredients, which I adminiftered to the K—g in his drink, and which had the effect of .weakening his nerves and of troubling his imagination. By thefe means I obtained a conftant fway over him, and this very artificial weaknefs proved the rod with which I chaftifed and governed him. I had moreover become a great proficient in the Machiavelian principles, and occafionally knew how to make ufe of them to my advantage. The rack, the whip, and banifhment, were lucky difcoveries, and ftood in the order of the day; and, however humane the K—g might be, however averfe from feverity, except in cafes of convicted guilt, I, neverthelefs, had through artifice and cunning fo far fucceeded, that every one trembled at the thoughts of my unlimited power, and yet blamed the K—g for its effects. Thus he was often, but as often unjuftly, called a tyrant; for he was in fact the moft juft, the moft humane, of princes. It was his weaknefs, of which I availed myfelf, that put him in this odious light, and my manner of treating the people caufed them to murmur and to complain. I would intercept letters, and by the aid of my helpmates had new ones forged; I likewife had orders of the cabinet diftributed. The Courts of Juftice, on my requeft, were forced to deliver up original deeds and papers, which I then arbitrarily committed to the flames. Through my Machiavelian arts, I obtained the fums that were requifite for the expences of my houfehold, my buildings, and travels. In fhort, every thing was at my command. This was the rage of the trumpeter's daughter.

Yet my pride was not fatisfied. It is obvious, that the Court, the nobility, and all the great people in the kingdom, muft hate me, though in public they would fhew me every mark of refpect; I knew this, and would be revenged. There happened to be a great *fête* at Court, at which none but the Royal Family and the moft diftinguifhed perfons among the nobility were to appear; that was to be the fcene of my vengeance. I prevailed upon the K—g to be permitted to appear at Court as Countefs of Lichtenau. General —— ufhered me in; I was dreffed in a royal robe, fhowered all over with diamonds and precious ftones. The Royal Family turned their backs upon me, and I was noticed by none but the courtiers. I was vexed, and complained to the K—g. " *Il faut faire bonne mine à mauvais jeu,*" faid he, and gently tapped my cheeks.

On the next morning my fteward brought me word, that all my fine furniture at my feat at Charlottenberg had been broken to pieces, the beds ripped open, and the coftly feathers of down ftrewed all over the rooms. I fufpected immediately who was the perpetrator, and brought my complaints before the K—g, who made up threefold for the lofs I had fuftained.

During my ftay at Franckfort, I formed an acquaintance with the Marquis Moufons, whom the revolution had compelled to leave France. He was both a fhrewd and a handfome man, almoft as cunning and as artful as Pinetti. At my requeft he was made reader to the K—g; he was a perfect mafter of the art of diverting the monarch's *ennui* and ill temper through his wit and humour, and through that frivolity which has fallen particularly to the lot of the French. He courted my affections, but with fuch refpect and fubmiffion as were a thoufand times more flattering to me than the tendereft careffes of the moft enamoured fop. He gradually gained my confidence, and, at laft, a certain intimacy took place between us, which put me in the poffeffion of many a valuable fecret. He completed me in the fublime politics of Machiavel, and we formed and eftablifhed a fociety, to which none but fuch were admitted as had been rigoroufly tried. The principle members were B——, W——, H——, H——, O——, B——, A——, G——, P—— du B——, R——; myfelf and Moufons were permanent prefidents.

Our orders were executed by my brother and a relation of mine, one Kunaſſius, a huntſman, and the watchman of our aſſembly.

Here are a few of the articles which Mouſons had drawn up, and which every member was obliged to keep ſacred on his oath.

The firſt law of all was the moſt inviolate ſecrecy, and rather to ſuffer to have the tongue cut out than betray a ſingle ſecret of the ſociety.

All the members that were choſen muſt promiſe to watch every one with whom they ſhould happen to have any intercourſe, and to liſten attentively to all their diſcourſes. 'To report faithfully, and in writing, to me and Mouſons, all they had obſerved and heard. They were to inſinuate themſelves into the Courts of Judicature, and every now and then to undertake little trips into the country, in order to diſcover what was going forward there, either to our advantage or diſadvantage. This arrangement enabled me to be informed of every thing that happened in the cabinet of the K---g, the miniſters, and the generals; to know all the verdicts given in the different departments of the law and police, as alſo all the orders iſſued in every regiment. I was acquainted with the ſecrets of every family, nay, with the temper of almoſt every individual perſon, and, of courſe, might take my meaſures accordingly.

Each member had, for the private uſe of his correſpondence, the following figures or cyphers:

12, 11, 10, 9, 8, 7, 6, 5, 4, 3, 2, 1, 13, 14, 15,
a, b, c, d, e, f, g, h, i, k, l, m, n, o, p,

16, 17, 18, 19, 20, 21, 22, 23, 24.
q, r, s, t, u, w, x, y, z.

If any of our letters had been intercepted, it ſtill would, with theſe precautions, have been difficult to unravel their contents. Beſides the above cyphers, Monſons, I, and B————, had other different ſets of figures, which we changed from time to time, and as circumſtances would require.

Our principles admitted aſſaſſination, ſuicide, poiſoning, murder, perjury, treaſon, rebellion, and, in ſhort, all the means which *prejudiced men* have termed crimes.

Much leſs obedience was to be ſhewn to the K—g and the laws than to me. And ſhould any one preſume to adhere to the K—g and the magiſtrates rather than to me, he muſt be cruſhed, as it was the caſe with E—— and the architect B————.

A general confufion in the government muft, of courfe, increafe the extent of my power, and, therefore, it was our grand object to excite diftruft in the K—g againft his fubjects, in the minifters againft their fubalterns, and in the counfellors againft their own colleagues. No power could fave the man who fhewed me the leaft fhadow of neglect or contempt.

We had found means to bribe thofe who were employed at the poft-offices in the country-towns, and they would let us have certain letters, which we either deftroyed or opened and fealed again, without its being vifible.

We even had our emiffaries in foreign countries, who were to endeavour to get admittance to the houfes of the great, of the foreign minifters, and the rich merchants, with a view of exciting diffention between the rulers of thofe refpective countries and their fubjects, between parents and children, and between the moft intimate friends. They were to form cabals, invent calumnies, roufe hatred and fufpicion againft any thing that did not agree with our plan, and to perfecute our antagonifts with poifon and dagger. Religion itfelf was not to be fpared when our welfare required it fo. They were to feize every opportunity to interfere with politics, to excite commotions, to preach rebellion, and through bribery to work up the people to revolt.

By means of this extended connexion, my power became fo immenfe; by this I carried every thing. It was this that made the world wonder how, with her withered charms, the Countefs of Lichtenau could manage to lead the K—g which way fhe chofe. The end fanctifies the means, faid my great tutor, Machiavel, and Moufons would analyze this doctrine with me in its moft minute details. He likewife was the man who initiated me into the myfteries of the God and the Goddefs of Love, and let me into fuch fecrets as no man before him had yet opened to my eyes. Oh! this Moufons was a great genius! and his gallantry was the true gallantry of a Frenchman.

I fucceeded in perfuading the K——g that the ufe of the waters of Pyrmont would prove highly beneficial to his health.

Moufons wrote to Hamburgh for a fet of French players; every kind of amufement imaginable was thought of to entertain the monarch. He fuffered, indeed, inexpreffibly from a pectoral dropfy. Pyrmont was converted into paradife upon earth; we had balls, operas, fire-works, caffinos, fuppers, dinners, breakfafts, horfe-races. All turned round the K—g in a perpetual circle of diverfion, and the fair fex particularly ftrove to attract the eye of the illuftrious gueft.

I there, likewife, had a little adventure, which particularly concerned myfelf. The Prince of W————, the proprietor of Pyrmont, fell deeply in love with me, and made me a formal propofal of marriage. I had refolved to exchange the title of a Countefs for that of a Princefs, and things had gone fo far that I had even obtained the K—g's permiffion for the purpofe. But fome minifter, who, at an ominous hour, diffuaded him from the purchafe of Pyrmont, threw fuch obftacles in my way, as entirely blafted this glorious marriage. I would have been revenged of him, had not the fudden weaknefs of the K—g haftened our departure for Potfdam.

I left Pyrmont with a heavy heart, and with a ftill heavier heart I arrived, in the K—g's company, at the Marble-palace, at Potfdam. Oh! could I have the leaft notion that this journey was to put an end to all my glory? Was it poffible for me to have the remoteft fhadow of a dream, that the powerful, the adored, the immortalized, the dreaded, Countefs of Lichtenau, like an abject criminal, fhould be kept in clofe confinement, in the very fame palace where, fovereign like, fhe dictated laws to a mighty monarch, and a mighty people, that had fo often groaned under the weight of her oppreffive defpotifm? Could I have thought to fee myfelf fome time fcoffed at, derided, and defpifed, by enemies, who rejoiced at my downfall, and to whom the clank of my chains is the harmony of mufic? To fee myfelf the object of fatire and abufe in all the newfpapers, pamphlets, ballads, and other vile pub- lications, in which my fame, my rank, and title, are traduced with unparallelled licentioufnefs? Could I have thought that my divine, my deareft- beloved Moufons, he, the prototype and mirror of the virtues of all the French emigrants, loaded with irons, fhould be dragged a prifoner to the fortrefs of Magdeburg? Alas! my journey to Pyr- mont proved the tomb of my glory; the divine mufic which I heard in that enchanting fcene of diffipation was converted into a mournful dirge to attend my bier. Thofe whom I have oppreffed and wantonly tormented now rife againft me, and loudly proclaim their own wrongs, and the infamy of the proftitute that fquandered away the little product of their hard money, and carried millions into foreign countries. The found of their cries ftrikes my ear with double horror, for, alas! it is the voice of truth!

Until the K—g's death, I never dreamed things would go fo far with me; hence I kept up my

ufual mode of living, and, together with my affociates, had nothing elfe in view but to amufe the
Monarch. He was frequently fubjeft to a tempo-
rary abfence of mind, and experienced, befides,
the moft unpleafant fymptoms of body. To
affuage the one and the other, I ufed to adminifter
to him corroborating draughts and narcotic pow-
ders. Alas! I did not know that I was bufily
employed in laying the fpeedy foundation of my
own ruin, for thefe very medicines tended to en-
feeble his conftitution, and, inftead of reftoring
health, had the contrary effeft, which was daily
vifible. The vivacity of Moufons, the gambols
of my dancing nymphs and fportive Naïades were
called into affiftance to diffipate the clouds that
fettled on the Sovereign's brow, to do which myfelf
I had the power no more.

As the K—g had been ordered to take much
exercife, I ufed to accompany him in a fmall tri-
umphal car, in which he took frequent airings in
the gardens of the Marble-palace. The accefs to
his perfon had been ftriftly forbidden, and I had
the fole and uninterrupted enjoyment of his prefence. At that time I difpatched Moufons to
Hamburgh with fome fecret papers, which I had
found in the red pocket-book, with direftions to
communicate them to Lord ——, who was then
at that place. Thefe papers confifted of the fecret

articles of the peace which had been concluded with France; they anfwered my purpofe exceedingly well, and I was paid for them with a good round fum of E———h g———. Curfed pocket-book! thou art the caufe of my misfortune; I have to thank thee for my confinement. Hadft thou not been difcovered in my poffeffion, what could the new K——g have urged againft the Countefs of Lichtenau? Perhaps my being the K——g's miftrefs. Who had a right to interfere with that? Who dared to find fault with that? Had not the Rev. Dr. H———, one of the ecclefiaftical board, a few years ago, openly declared, that the country ought to vote thanks to the Countefs of Lichtenau for promoting the purity of the Chriftian religion? But I am guilty of a crime againft the ftate; I am guilty of high treafon; there lies the rub; there the caufe of my anxiety, and my fear of imprifonment for life. Hence the remorfe that preys on my mind day and night, and which deprives me of fleep and reft in the gloomy walls of my prifon.

By the joint advice of Moufons and Rietz, I gave the K——g a *fête*, the gaiety of which was to furpafs every thing. The fpot pitched upon for this purpofe was one of thofe gardens at Potfdam which we called the Englifh gardens, and in which the beauties and the deformities of nature are all colleƐed and contrafted with each other on a few acres of land. This fpot was kept under lock and key by one of the trufty guards of the affociation. My Naïades, Cupids, Sylphs, and Nymphs, fcarcely veiled with tranfparent gauze, opened this divertifement, and the firft beauties were felected to heighten the glowing fcene. After the pantomime commenced a ball.

A ball, it is well known, is a great promoter of voluptuoufnefs. One couple after the other difappeared; whole groupes were feen fcattered about in the moft lafcivious attitudes; here a Dido in the embraces of an Æneas; there a Cleopatra, loft in an ocean of delight with her tender Antony. Little Cupids, in half-lighted grottos, by the twinkling ray of an expiring torch, prepared the hymeneal feaft, in which the God of Love, the hero of the piece, exerted his talents in the moft enamoured manner.

I walked hand in hand with the K——g through thefe enchanting fcenes, and explained to him the meaning of the various groups. Beautiful! excellent! delightful! exclaimed he repeatedly. What a charming woman thou art, Minna! One of the dancers, a pretty little girl, whom I had initiated into all the myfteries of love, and whom the K——g was particularly partial to, attended us on our promenade, and, on a fignal agreed between us, conducted him to a bower, the moft enchanting that imagination can·paint. The King would fit down upon the green, when on a fudden it opened, and prefented a beautiful fopha with cufhions, over which an elegant baldachin of flowers was fuf-pended, in wreaths and feftoons. At a convenient diftance I had placed a male and a female finger, who were to reprefent a love-fcene, and to accompany their amourous attitudes with fongs expreffive of their paffions; a little farther off another voice echo-like repeated the fweet accents, whilft at a ftill greater diftance the liquid founds of a German flute died on the love-fick breeze, and threw the foul into that kind of penfive melancholy which generally leads to the moft exquifite delights. The fongfter began, the flute warbled, the echo repeated, the tune was fo heart-melting, the words fo tender, the fituation fo novel, the King fo preffing———.

This was the laft tender fcene in which we were engaged; for a few days afterwards his health declined vifibly, and he was unable to leave his bed. Even on his fick couch, Moufons ftrove to foothe his melancholy and his pain through well-chofen amufements, but all in vain. The machine was deranged, and ftopped at the very moment when I leaft expected it.

The man was now gone that raifed me from nothing, and fhowered favours on me; that fun was
fet in whofe luftre I fhone with borrowed light.
The veil fell off, and, feized with horror and remorfe, I at once funk again into my original infigni-
ficancy. I fhook as if I had been touched by the
chilling hand of death, and fcarce had recollection
enough to defire Moufons to order poft-horfes,
to empty the King's ftrong box, and to take poffeffion of his large diamond and his pocket-book.
At that inftant an officer entered with twenty-four
men, and informed me, that, by order of the new
King, I was his prifoner. Moufons was immediately taken into cuftody, and within twenty-four
hours tranfported to Magdeburg. Thunderftruck,
I ftared at the officer, collected all the effrontery
I ftill could mufter, and, with a haughty counte-
nance and tone of voice, afked him, Who dared
to arreft a Countefs?---No one but the Emperor
dared do fo.

The Officer.—It may be fo; but at prefent I
have the order of the King my mafter, which
both you and I muft obey. Should the King be
miftaken, and wrong you, Madam, I am fure he
will give you ample fatisfaction.

I was a prifoner; my papers were fealed up;
the curfed pocket-book and the King's ring were

taken from me, and a felect committee were appointed to examine my treafonable practices againft the King and his fubjects. I am criminal before my own confcience; I am fo in the eye of the law. To whom muft I appeal? Who will protect the wretch who thus has outraged humanity? Who can fave me? and what have I to expect? Mercy alone I muft have recourfe to, and what will not mercy do? What is mercy but to forgive the criminal? And is not forgivenefs the moft glorious prerogative of regal power? I own my crimes are boundlefs; they call to Heaven for vengeance, —but all may be well yet; the King is juft—but he is merciful—and I am a frail woman!

ORIGINAL PAPERS

OF THE

COUNTESS LICHTENAU,

COMMONLY CALLED

MINNA ENCKE.

I ᴀᴍ with child, mother, and big F——— is ready to die with joy about it. But he is fond of variety. About eight days fince there came an Italian ftrumpet here from Leipfic; I think her name is Saporetti; that curfed pander, that Frenchman, Dufour, has introduced her to him. She has been repeatedly with the Prince at Potfdam, fo Rietz has told me. But patience only; I'll contrive to let the King know, and then all her ⋅fine plans will be defeated; out of the kingdom with her in a hurry! The King, I am informed, a few days ago, faid, If my nephew cannot live without a w———e, I fhould prefer to fee him keep a German to a foreigner; the latter are much more expenfive, and may fome time difcover and reveal fecrets of the State. Your powder, mother, does wonders; whenever F—— has taken a dofe of it, he is quite amorous, and loads me with careffes and favours. Let him think what he pleafes, fay I to myfelf, provided I can retain my powers over him. Yefterday George brought me a fine watch, fet with brilliants, bracelets, and ear-rings of the fame, a ftomacher, and a fuperb necklace, with a medallion containing the Prince's portrait. Herewith I fent you thirty Frederics-d'ors for my brother; I have created him my equerry; he is to difpatch my letters to Potf-dam, and muft have a good poney, whofe oats and furniture are my concern.

The King has been pleafed to fend Madam Saporetti, well attended, out of the land, and given orders to look after Monfieur Dufour. He keeps himfelf concealed at Berlin, and, to elude all inquiry, has taken the name Chofieu. The Prince has not the leaft notion of all this being my doings, and is as tender and as loving as ever. Rietz himfelf is very glad to fee that French puppy in the dumps, for who knows but he might fome time have got him out of his mafter's favour, for he is full of intrigue, and then all would be over with every one of us. Rietz is a good kind of ftupid fellow, all on my fide, and feems to be pleafed to fee the Prince fo conftant in his love to me.

—————————

THE Prince abfolutely infifts upon my marriage with Rietz, becaufe fince the late difcovery the King is angry with him. It is only intended to be a mere farce to outwit the old fox, who, as he is paft all enjoyment, would have others infenfible to every pleafure to keep him company.

I fhall be obliged to fwallow the bitter draught, and permit his Highnefs's fhoe-black to call me his wife. Krantz has inferted a moft biting epigram againft me in his weekly publication; it alludes to my former calling, when I ufed to fell lemons and oranges. Curfe the fool! fend him four Frederics-d'ors, and he will hold his tongue, I warrant you; he is nothing but a hungry fcribbler, that for money would convert angels into devils, and devils into angels of light.

—————————

SINCE the laft review in Silefia, the King is extremely fufpicious and ill-tempered with the Prince, and all our party. He has him watched as clofely as poffible, and knows every one that comes and goes. My dear F———c can only vifit me by night; he comes on horfeback, changes his horfes at Zehlendorf, and leaves me at three in the morning. At five he is back at Potfdam, and every morning appears on the parade to avoid fuf-picion. The King has fent Forçade for a foldier to a regiment at Brieg, becaufe, as he pleafes to term it, he affilts his nephew in all his little fro-lics. The Prince is extremely chagrined at it, and has confoled poor Forçade with the profpect of better times. This may, probably, have induced him, in his fits of ill humour, to vent his rage on poor Rietz, whom, of late, he has feveral times treated to a royal caning. There are two Sile-fian Counts at Berlin, of the name of Wingerfky; the Prince is very intimate with them. Who are thofe fellows? My brother muft watch them, and let me know.

Werner, of Breflau, and Eckftein, of Schmie-berg, have brought money. The rich convents of thofe places have granted a joint loan, which the Prince has promifed to repay them on his acceffion to the throne. They are pretty good people. This Werner and this Eckftein have paid me a vifit to-day, together with Rietz.

THE old grumbler walks upon his laſt legs, and, by what Selle and Zimmermann have told the Prince, he cannot hold out above three weeks longer, and then who is to interrupt our career? O! the pretty caſks full of gold which lie in the cellars underneath the old palace at Berlin! We will bring them to light. Then we command, do any thing I chuſe, and I'll turn him about till I find the right handle of him. Now we ſhall ſoon want a ſet of confidential perſons to aſſiſt us with counſel and deed; for, alas! what do we know about government and politics? Werner and Bender are two men that will do for me; they know better than I what they are about.

———————

THESE laſt three weeks have been monſtrous long; every hour we expected to receive the news of his death. But he is gone at laſt; between two and three this morning the old grumbler breathed his laſt, and my F——c is King. Only think, mother, F——c is King! Minna now will govern, and from this very inſtant a new proſpect begins to open to us. I am going to buy a houſe Unter den Linden *. I mean to fill it

* A ſtreet in Berlin, ſo called from the plantation of lime-trees laid out there.

with entire new furniture, which shall not be a whit inferior to that of the Queen's. Werner has been made minister, and Bender has obtained the commission of a major-general and adjutant. These are two of our creatures, do you see, who will work our good-natured K—g nicely.

THE King has, a few days since, paid repeated visits to the Dowager-Queen; and my spies tell me, that he is extremely smitten with the beauty of Miss V———*, who, in fact, has been the only

* Mademoiselle Voss has a kind of natural wit, some information, is rather more wilful than firm, and is very obviously aukward, which she endeavours to disguise by assuming an air of simplicity. She is ugly, and that even to a degree; and her only excellence is the goodness of her complexion, which I think rather wan than white, and a fine neck; over which she threw a double handkerchief the other day, as she was leaving Prince Henry's comedy, to cross the apartments, saying to the Princess Frederica, " I must take good care of them, for it is after these they run." It is this mixture of eccentric licentiousness (which she accompanies with airs of ignorant innocence) and vestal severity, which the world says has seduced the King. Mademoiselle Voss, who holds it ridiculous to be German, and who is tolerably well acquainted with the English language, affects the Anglomania to excess, and thinks it a proof of politeness not to love the French. Her vanity, which has found itself under restraint, when in company with some amiable people of that nation, hates those it cannot imitate, more especially because her sarcasms are returned with interest. Thus, for instance, the other day I could

caufe of all thefe vifits. All our engines are at play to extinguifh this flame, and if I cannot bring that about, I am loft for ever! All this is a court-cabal to get me *out*, and one of the nobility *in*. Some people, by this means, hope to acquire greater influence in the affairs of the State. Mifs V——, I am told, has a pretty face, and, what is ftill worfe, fhe is faid to be extremely virtuous; the King will, therefore, be at fome trouble to fubdue her. The Dowager-Queen, a very godly princefs, keeps a fharp look out, and has, I am told, loudly expoftulated about it with the King.

My fpies watch every motion, and I am inftantaneoufly apprized of the moft minute occurrence. I don't know how it is, but fome time fince the King was extremely referved with me, and I

not keep filence when I heard an exclamation, " Oh, heavens! when fhall I fee, when fhall we have an Englifh play! I really fhould expire with rapture!" For my part, Madam, faid I drily, " I rather wifh you may not, fooner than you imagine, ftand in need of French plays." All thofe who began to be offended by her high airs, finiled ; and Prince Henry, who pretended not to hear her, laughed aloud. Her face was fuffufed with blufhes, and fhe did not anfwer a word, but it is eafy to punifh, difficult to correct.

She has hitherto declared open war againft the myftics, and detefts the daughters of the chief favourite, who are maids of honour to the Queen. But as amidft her weakneffes fhe is tranfported by devotion even to fuperftition, nothing may be depended on for futurity.——*Mirabeau's Secret Hiftory of the Court of Berlin.*

would lay my head that all this is on account of Mifs V——. But let me but once more lay hold of him, and your powder fhall do wonders, mother; he then fhall leave me no more, I warrant you. We have contrived matters fo, that my F———c, in the newfpapers, is called the dear beloved; he gives full credit to the appellation, and who knows but thofe that wrote this nonfenfe believed it to be true full as well as he does?

———————

Woe! woe! and three times woe! the great mifchief has begun. Mifs V—— has yielded, and is the King's favorite. Could you think of any thing fo exquifitely foolifh as this? She has given herfelf up to the King, on condition of having a left-handed marriage! The firft Court Chaplain and Member of the Confiftory, the Rev. H——, on Friday laft, performed the ceremony at the palace of Charlottenburg, for which he received a hundred glittering Frederics-d'ors. She is now formally Queen, on the left hand, and, in the moft extenfive meaning of the word, the ruling queen, for fhe governs even the King. Would you believe it, mother, a formal law has, by order of the King, been made concerning marriages on the left hand, and this law has been inferted in the code of laws with all the publicity, to give a fanction to this archicomical mock-marriage! The public laugh at it, make remarks, and no one follows this Don Quixotism. But, dear mother, what is to become of me? I muſt have the K--g, ſhould I tear him out of the arms of Proſerpine herſelf, ſhould I be forced to fetch him out of the midſt of heaven or of hell. He ſhall be mine, mine alone! Think of means, dear ſweet mother! No matter what means, no matter how dangerous! Neceſſity has no law; I muſt clear the road to the heart of my F————c; I will pull up by the root every thing that oppoſes me; V—— muſt vaniſh away from among the living. Aſk A—lang, Werner, Bender, and all our people, how I muſt ſet about it. I will have no denial; a third perſon is moſt fit for the buſineſs.

V—— is pregnant, and does not ſuffer the King to go from her ſide one minute. He is moſt vulgarly ſmitten with that little figure; he ſees nothing but through her eyes; he does nought but by her directions. They ſay, in town, that ſhe makes him do many a good action*; I know nothing of it.

---

* Literally true. Had this good and liberal ſoul lived longer, the ſweat of the brows of the ſubjects would not have been ſquandered away in ſo wanton a manner.

What do they call good? Is it, perhaps, that now he meddles with the concerns of the land, and reads every fcrap himfelf? Pray what has a King minifters for, and why does he pay them? Let thofe work, and let him be merry and amufe himfelf! State-affairs are much too tedious to interfere with them. As foon as I have him again, I will foon make him fenfible that my philofophy is the beft of all, and alone fuits a monarch. He fhall be no fecretary; not he, indeed; he fhall not daily ftain his fingers with ink, and fign nonfenfe. Rietz and M—— may do that. A-propos, let me foon know the pleafing intelligence, of which you gave me a hint not long fince. Aqua toffana won't do, dear mother, for we are not yet intimate enough with V—— to approach her thus. It ought to be a fubtile and expeditious remedy, fuch a one as will rid us of that fool without creating any fufpicion.

This moment Rietz comes to inform me, that the King has raifed Mifs V—— to a Countefs I——heim. He has fent her to-day, by Rietz, the Imperial diploma, together with a brilliant hair pin, of great value. For God's fake, fpeak with S—— about the matter, left you will have me lofe my fenfes.

Minna! Minna! only don't be fo violent. S—
has been bufy for us all. In the afternoon he will
fend you the box with the powder, you know,
and which has arrived from Venice only laft night.
F—— went thither poft, day and night, and ftopt
but one day at Vienna to take a little reft. It cofts
2000 zechins, but its effect is worth more than
2000 millions. But hufh and be clofe! and, for
God's fake, no more confidents!

———————

SHE is fafely gone to eternal reft, mother, and
we may again be tranquil. During the firft fortnight the King has been inconfolable, and would
fuffer nobody in his prefence, for he was actually
in love with the filly creature. But he will come
round again, I hope. To-morrow I give a *fête* at
Charlottenburg, and there I will mufter up what
charms I have to rivet the rambler for ever. Your
powder, dear mother, muft again do the bufinefs.
I have now good hopes all goes on to my wifhes.

LETTERS

FROM

VIENNA, ITALY, FRANCE, and PYRMONT*.

———————

ONE cannot know, my dear A——, what turn this may take with us, at the event of fome future change. I therefore, firſt of all, intend to take a trip to Piſa, as it is called, and there I'll contrive to place my property, which chiefly confiſts in good paper and jewels, as advantageouſly as I can. Let a change take place then, I don't care, for I know whither to direct my courſe. Pray let the pamphlet in queſtion be as biting as poſſible, for it is intended to produce effects. The people ſhall know that I am the favorite of the

———

* As the letters, and other writings of the Counteſs of Lichtenau, reach down to the French revolution and the expedition againſt that nation, but, having ſcarce any thing intereſting in them, except what concerns the amorous intrigues of an artful woman, the Editor has thought proper to omit all that commonplace ſtuff, to preſent the Reader with papers of greater importance.

King, their Sovereign, and that I was born to command. Rietz will purpofely deftroy every paper, and every propofal, that comes from that quarter. Werner and Bender have, likewife, difpofed the King in a manner, that he will accede to nothing that has not our fanction. He muft be amufed with all imaginable kinds of entertainments, that may tend to divert his mind fo that he may lofe all recollection of this bufinefs. He is bufy with projects concerning the Countefs of the Mark; he is looking out for a good match for the fweet creature. Many have already applied to me, wifhing to obtain my confent, but none of them would fuit. The magnificent monument of marble of Carrara, for my fon, is to be ready next week.

Pifa is an agreeable place, where you may amufe yourfelf like a Queen; notwithftanding which I fhall not ftay above four weeks. Pray tell Bender, M———, and Werner, to prepare the King againft my return. And what is that ftory about the Countefs D—hoff? I hope he is not in earneft with that creature; don't let things go fo far as they went with the Countefs I—heim. Let that be your care, dear A———. I have no objection if the King means nothing but a little amufement. At Vienna they are bufy with the Imperial diploma for me. Keep a good watch, and let me know.

———————

Dear little Rietz, I muft be feparated from you, for within fix weeks I fhall be a Countefs. Be affured, at the fame time, that all this will produce no alteration in our connexion. All fhall remain on the old footing; we only change names.

Believe me, good boy, you and I aft too confpicuous a part not to be envied. To filence the invidious, and to awe thofe who, through their exalted birth, might injure us, I am to be made Countefs Lichtenau. The Court of Vienna has great influence, and its protection may be of ufe to me. All the return they expeft for this is a mere trifle; nothing but an alliance againft France. I am to perfuade the King to it. When at Vienna I fhall mention more of this plan to A——, Werner, and Bender. Till then farewell, my good Rietz, and clear the King's lobbies of all thofe that can injure me in his affections.

———————

Friend A——, tell Bender that an exprefs from me will communicate a plan to him, by which

E

the King is to be perfuaded to undertake a journey to Pilnitz. The Court of Vienna then will fend an invitation to the King, and the Ch——r de S———— accepts the interview. Could not it be contrived at the fame time that the King goes to the review at Breflau? All muft be done within a fortnight. Vienna is an enchanting place, and it has more charms for me than Berlin itfelf; there are a thoufand varieties here. I am much courted by the great, and the letters the I————l ambaf-fador has furnifhed me with are all good. The Chancery of the Empire has orders to difpatch my diploma, without any further expence than the ufual fees paid on thofe occafions. The Emperor to-morrow fets out upon a journey to Bohemia, and feems to have the execution of fome grand plan in view. Only perfuade Bender to an in-terview at Pilnitz; we muft furnifh the King with amufement.

THE courier of the camp has brought me the King's invitation to Pilnitz. He has been pre-fented with 200 ducats by the Emperor, and I have given him a gold repeater. Some of thefe days I go by Prague to Drefden, where elegant lodgings are prepared for me at the Hotel de Saxe. The intelligence that the Countefs D—hoff has incurred the King's difpleafure, and that G—fet has been ordered out of the country, has filled me with extacy; it is mufic to my ears. Bender and Werner are actually great men; indeed I did not take them to be mafters of fo much art and addrefs. An excellent idea, to make the King believe that they intended to poifon him! Now he can efcape us no more, fhould he even wifh it.

———

FROM DRESDEN.

HERE we have a continual round of pleafures and entertainments. However fhort the meeting at Pilnitz might be, yet there was a variety of the moft brilliant *fêtes*. Fireworks, illuminations, balls, an Italian opera buffa, in rapid fucceffion, and I enjoyed it indeed. Leopold is gone to Prague to be crowned King of Bohemia; the King will ftay one day longer. I have not been able to converfe above twice with him; he was continually befet by the French emigrants, and the brother of the King of France. The campaign is refolved on, and we are allied with Auftria. If the French do not chufe to let us have our way, our plan is to march ftrait to Paris, and to affift the Emperor to conquer Alface and Lorrain. As an equivalent the King is to have Dantzic, Thorn, and a great part of Poland. All this, do you fee, dear A——lany, has been but a ftroke of the pen.

In eight days, at fartheſt, we are at Paris, and attend at the King's grand opera. Verdun has not coſt us a ſingle man, and I am here theſe eight days. *Voilà la maitreſſe declarée du Roi de P—e,* ſay the French, as they ſurvey me with a glance from top to toe. But let me reach Paris, dear A——lang, and you ſhall hear of me. Have you heard the news, that by my management the K—g has ordered lodgings for Dufour in the fortreſs of Magdeburg? That infamous raſcal wrote from this place to his friends at Berlin. That vulgar gang would beſet the K—g without intermiſſion, and follow him even to France. Fine encomiums on the Pruſſian arms, indeed! It luckily happened, that the letter fell into my hands; I communicated it to the K—g at a favorable moment, and he ſent him to Magdeburg. There he may continue his remarks on my journey to France as long as he ſhall think proper. I am glad to be rid, at laſt, of that curſed ſneaking raſcal.

We retreat as faſt as we can; for our fine project of penetrating to Paris through Champagne has altogether miſcarried. Dumourier has had an interview with the Prince and Count K—uth, after which our retreat was immediately reſolved on. I travel through Limburg and Treves ſtrait to Frankfort, and there wait for further news from you. I have again ſent half a million of dollars,

in Frederic-d'ors, to my agent in London, and expect a frefh cargo from Berlin. I am, upon the
whole, well pleafed with the Englifh; they are a
charming nation.

I AM extremely concerned at what you tell
me about the difturbances. which have taken place
at Breflau on account of the Privy Counfeller
Werner, for you know how much we ftand in-
debted to him. The deputies from Breflau have
been introduced to the K—g here at Franckfort.
His M——y has very gracioufly received them,
and perfonally attended at the report which they
made of the whole tranfaction. He is extremely
difpleafed with Werner, and mean while has fuf
pended him from his office. Pray, dear A—lang,
fee what you can do in poor Werner's behalf; he
has an amazing number of enemies. As often as
I take an opportunity to fpeak of him to the K—g,
his anfwer always is, " Do not intercede for that
fellow, he is a downright wretch." I am told,
that the accounts received from South Pruffia will
have great influence upon the fpeedy return of the
K—g. Rietz has received letters from Werner
and I——ger, befides two addreffes to the K—g,
which he will tender him this day; they may,
perhaps, produce fome good effect, for he is in a
good humour.

E 3

GET my palace ready, for I fhall fet off for Berlin before the K—g. He goes to South Pruffia, and returns to Berlin by the way of Silefia; L—fini and B--werder are his only attendants. There muft have arrived very important difpatches from Peterfburg, for the cabinet is bufy without interruption. The K—g has this day fignified, both to the army and the different foreign minifters who are prefent at head-quarters, that he means to leave the army on the Rhine, and to repair to South Pruffia. The Prince of Naffau has already waited on me feveral times, and yefterday made me a prefent of a magnificent cloke, of the moft exquifite Ruffian fur.

A SERIES of letters follow, very little interefting; fuch as thoughts on the journey to Pifa, of the ufual caft; a projeét for marrying the Countefs of the Mark, her daughter; letters to du Bofk, Bauman, Wollner, Amelang, Schmidts, Rietz, Guldling, Granfort, &c.; forged cabinet-papers, cypher-writing, and chemical receipts; fome Italian direétions to ufe the aqua toffana, and other poifonous preparations; love-letters from feveral fools, among which there is even a *déclaration d'amour* of the Prince of W———k, from Pyrmont; intercepted letters, direéted partly to the K—g and his minifters, partly to other Sovereigns and great men; a projeEt of a loan for the K—g, to which, likewife, belong the fhares in the adminiftration of the tobacco, that unfortunately mifcarried; twelve blanks, with the fignature of the K—g and the cabinet-feal.

PRAY, dear A———, enquire who has had the audacity to deftroy my fine furniture at Charlottenburg, and to throw all my plate into the Spree, whilft I attended at the marriage of the hereditary Prince L————is. You may well be furprifed to hear of my being at Court; but who could refufe the Countefs of Lichtenau? I have a notion that the outrage has been committed by officers, who were countenanced by the h————y P————. for otherwife, how could the guard at the palace have permitted it, without giving the alarm? The K—g has promifed me fatisfaEtion, and the fcoundrels fhall run the gauntlet. May thofe female fools burft with fpite! I don't care; the K—g is mine for ever!

At my little domeftic theatre I'll give to-morrow a moft extraordinary *fête*, to which none but ladies of my acquaintance are invited. Every one is to appear in a light airy drefs. The performance is to open with an Italian piece, called Hymen's Wake. Some male and female dancers are to perform, on this occafion, in the ufual mode. After the theatrical reprefentation there is to be a grand ball, in fuch a ftile as cannot fail to captivate the fenfes; after which I have prepared an enchanting grotto for the K—g. I have inftructed little Schult, the dancer, how to behave; fhe is to re-prefent a Venus. There is a *fête* for you! The K—g, not long ago, faid to me, " What a charming woman you are, Minna! You facrifice your own health to promote mine."

PYRMONT, IN 1797.

THE K—g actually means to purchafe Pyrmont in right earneft, and negociations on the fubject are carried on with great activity. That little tract of country is incumbered with heavy debts; its produce is about 200,000 dollars a-year. The P——e de ———— has made me a ferious tender of his hand, and thinks, by that means, to clear his eftate. The titles of Princefs and your Royal Highnefs, I muft confefs, have great charms for me. But then I cannot move in fo extenfive a circle as formerly, on account of my great dif-tance from Berlin. What would you have me do, A——lang? The French players at Hamburg have been called to this place; they are to have 500 Frederics d'ors for their journey hither, and as many on their return to Hamburg. The K—g fuffers a great deal from his pectoral dropfy, that makes us think of fuch a variety of amufements for him. Between you and me, I am alarmed for his health. Even the Englifh Doctor often fhrugs up his fhoulders, and gives but very faint hopes. If I can but bring about one thing, he may then depart in peace. My emigrant, Coller, is exactly the man we want; next week I fend him to Hamburg with the papers in queftion, and I hope he will do bufinefs properly, and prove ufeful to us. My brother and Kunaffius are to accompany him.

Here follows a Number of Letters addreffed to her Mother, out of which the following are felected:

I am quite impatient to write to my deareft mother; I have fo much to fay that I don't know when I fhall have done, but I muft tell my deareft mother every thing, and then my mind will be at eafe. I have had fome dreadful dreams; pray Heaven that all be right. You muft affift me with your advice; you muft take care to difcover every thing that is faid of me; we muft do every thing to retain our power and influence; I know the people hate me becaufe I hate them. If there are any lampoons handed about in fecret, you muft procure them, and find out, if poffible, the authors. You know I have every thing to dread from my own fex. Paris is an enchanting city; fuch a continued round of pleafures, balls, operas, and dances;—and, then, fuch gallantry. You cannot conceive how my toilet is frequented by perfons of the fiift rank, and how my charms are admired! But, O my dear mother, you cannot conceive how my pride is humbled as often as I think of the lownefs of my birth! Sometimes I am like to faint when I think of it, but I banifh it from my thoughts as faft as I can. What do titles, and .beauty, and fplendour, and power, avail? After all, I am but the daughter of a trumpeter; but K————fe has been of great fervice to me in this refpeft, for he has whifpered, under the feal of fecrecy, that I am the daughter of Baron de S————ts, by a left-handed marriage. This ftory muft be kept alive, and you muft nod affent to it; and if a letter or two could be forged, it would ftamp it with credit. Confult L.—e on this, but if it is not managed with the greateft addrefs, it will make things worfe than ever; let me be the daughter of any one rather than the daughter of a trumpeter. I have fent Krebs purpofely with this letter; you may truft him. The French women drefs to the higheft advantage, and Gleim tells me, that fome of the firft judges of beauty fay that I am ten times handfomer than the Countefs du Barry was in her fineft days. I fend you a portrait of her, that you may judge, for I know my dear mother will not deceive me. Gleim is a charming fellow, but I muft not truft him too far, though he thinks he is in full poffeffion of all my fecrets; he is a vain fellow, but he is a charming fellow for all that. I am often complimented on my accent, and the Abbé de Lille affured me the other morning, that I might be miftaken for a French woman. In that refpeѐt, this was a high compliment, for the French are the vaineft creatures on earth. I had fome verfes fent me a few days ago, but the fcribbler deceived me, for I find they were written fome years ago by Voltaire, on Madame de Pompadour; you cannot conceive how it mortified me. Then, as to my age, I think I may venture to ftrike off three years; how do I tremble at the idea of wrinkled cheeks! Give me youth, beauty, and birth; thefe are all I afk, and then I will hold my lover as long as I pleafe, or, if I fhould lofe him, I can foon replace him. O dear mother! I have one queftion to afk, and I tremble when I afk it. Are you fure I had the fmall-pox? Surely I hope I had. I have luckily got acquainted with a woman who excels in all kinds of cofmetics, and other fecrets of great importance. I muft purchafe them all, coft what they will. You cannot conceive how I am putting your leſſons in practice, and ſuccefsfully too; ſometimes I affect ſilence, loſt in thought, and counterfeit indiſpoſition, that I may read the effects in the eyes of certain perſons. The French excel in all kinds of intrigue; every man is a lover, and talks of ſentiment, but be aſſured, my dear mother, that real paſſion never yet found its way into the heart of a Frenchman. I have ſeen the handſome Ferſon twice; he paſſes for the richeſt man in Sweden; he lives in great ſplendour, but, at the ſame time, with the greateſt œconomy. Pougent has promiſed to give me ſome leſſons in muſic; he is natural ſon to the Prince of Conti. Would that I could ſay I was natural daughter to ſome prince, or any perſon that could boaſt of noble blood! and yet I think there is ſome in my veins; it is impoſſible I can be the daughter of a trumpeter; you know I bear no reſemblance to him. You ſee how this ſits on my heart; I can ſay any thing to you. I do not know how long I ſhall remain in Paris. I have bought a number of pictures; one day they ſhall adorn my *Chateau*. They have been choſen by an Italian, who is ſaid to be a great connoiſſeur in that line, but the Italians are great cheats. Do not detain Krebs long; ſend him to me with good news. I wiſh you could ſee me, I never looked ſo charming in my life. Pray tell me if poor Elmenbent is alive;

if she is, you muſt give her ſome money; she knows my age, and she may blab it with other ſecrets. As to * * * * * * * * *

Krebs will tell you how I am adored. You muſt not let him be near my ſiſter, for the Count might aſk him ſome queſtions, and you know how aukward he is in his anſwers. I have not time to finiſh this letter; I muſt dreſs for the opera. Write, write all, and ſend Krebs back on the wings of impatience. * * * * * * *

O my dear angelic mother! I read your letter over with ſuch joy, that I thought I ſhould faint at every line. You know, you may ſay, you got acquainted with the Baron at Eldagſen; he paſſed a couple of years there, and, if the ſtory is well managed, who is to contradict it. I am more afraid of Paſtor Beſſer than any, but he muſt be bribed or flattered with the hopes of preferment. I think we will contrive to manage this matter to our ſatisfaction. I am forming a little party here, but it is hard to truſt the French, for, notwithſtanding all the appearance of levity which they aſſume, they are full of deſign, and, though they are always ſpeaking, yet they are always thinking. For all that, I have purchaſed the ſecret of the coſmetic; its divine! I cannot tell you the enchanting effect of it; but this is the only ſecret I muſt keep from my dear mother and fifter. By the bye, you muft not let her fee one of my letters; you know fhe could never keep a fecret fince fhe was born. Above all, how does my heart rejoice when you tell me I had the frightful fmall-pox! You are quite fure of it, you muft not deceive; but you did not tell me when, becaufe I would ftrive to recolleft. You muft get Candidate Bang to write fome verfes on me; the Prince reads every thing that he writes; tell him that I never looked fo lovely in my life; do not let him forget my teeth, and eyes, and fine hair, and, above all, my fmile; but, if he fhould fpeak of my mind, let that be artlefs and innocent; but, above all, let him praife my conftancy in love; let him draw me in the midft of a circle of dying lovers, with my eyes fixed on one only. Do not let him know that I defired this, for he is one of thofe that cannot keep a fecret either, but we muft make ufe of fuch perfons at times; he is a fool with all his learning, but we will keep that to ourfelves. Only three lampoons, dear mother; I think I know their author, and, inftead of being paid, he fhall pay for them. They feem to be at a lofs what to fay of me here; but I am afraid, though they bow in my prefence, that they fneer behind my back. I have got acquainted with Count Beincourt; he has got an immenfe eftate in Normandy, and one of the oldeft families in that

country. Oh! what it is to be defcended of an old family! There are fome that affeft to defpife it, but I know that they wifh for it in fecret. I have met with two or three Roficrufians, but not one Swedenborgian. Do you know that I go by the name of the handfome Swedenborgian? I had a frightful dream this morning; I dreamed that *
* * * * * * * * * * * * * *
* * * * * * * * * * * * * *
* * * * * * * * * * * * * *
I can tell any thing to you. Pray, my dear mother, tell it under a feigned name. I fhould like to pay a vifit to England, becaufe I am told the nobility in that country are not fo proud as ours; notwithftanding this, Heaven knows what money, they fpend in Paris; they are fine looking men, but fpeak very bad French. The French admire nothing of the Englifh but their conftitution, but I admire their opennefs. Gofs has taught me to fpeak a little Englifh, but it is a horrid language to pronounce. I muft learn fome Italian before I fet out for Italy. Did Krebs tell you what happened in Champagne? A ftupid carman drove againft my carriage, and overturned it; I got into fuch a paffion that I ftruck the fellow twice. It was fome time before I could get the carriage repaired, for the French are mere bunglers at any thing of the kind; it will, however, be a good apology for me to get an Englifh carriage. You

muſt find out what Baron Hertzberg ſays; every thing that comes from his lips has great weight; but he is too buſy with his mulberry-trees to mind the trumpeter's daughter. Oh! how does that horrid word chill my veins! Krebs is a faithful fellow, but I am afraid he has mentioned ſomething about the bathing ſcene; it runs in my mind he has. I am afraid to mention it to him, leſt I ſhould get into a paſſion, and then I might ſay ſomething that would ruin us all. I do not know what they think of me at Deſſau; there I know I am hated and envied; Bekker can tell you, but I know it already; I am hated and envied in that vile place, but they do not know all, and that is a conſolation. Let us make out our own ſtory, and when it is properly done, we will ſet them all at defiance. Send the interpretation of my dream. Be kind to Krebs, he is a faithful fellow, and that is all he is good for.

My deareſt mother! the very firſt line of your letter revived my ſpirits. The interpretation of my dream is delightful, but the very thoughts of the black dog freezes the blood in my veins; yet a dream is but a dream, but then they come to paſs,—" My power is but in its infancy!" Oh! that is too flattering! If that is the caſe, I will yet be revenged of all my enemies. As to the people, a little money will make friends of them at any time, and money fhall not be fpared when I have an objeĉt in view. Baron S——ts will not do; he is ftill alive, and at prefent on a tour in Lapland. I wifh they could change him into a rein deer; but we muft think of fomebody elfe. What do you think of Count L——d; his family is ancient; he is old and vain of his amours. Secrecy is all; if I am able to retain ————, I will laugh at every thing. I affeĉt a total indifference to politics, but they little know that it engroffes all my attention. O heavens! what a figure I fhall cut when I return! How my drefs will be imitated, and all my airs and motions fought after and copied! Veftris gives me fome leffons. I negleĉt nothing that may render me charming in the eyes of ————; that is my grand objeĉt. O dear mother, let me know every thing that you hear! do not fpare money; there is nothing can be done without. Lu——ini, I am afraid, is gaining ground every day in a certain ————; I dread the very name of an Italian. I tell you a Frenchman or Italian has more art in his little finger than fifty Germans put together. My very looks are watched in this place, but I think I can cheat them even in that. When they talk of politics, I pretend that I know nothing of the matter; yet it is the moft difficult thing in the world to deceive a Frenchman or a

French woman. The Marquis de la F——e is a ſtupid fellow; I do not know how the deuce he has acquired ſo much popularity. Mirabeau is an artful man; I muſt be civil to him, as he is writing ſomething, and, perhaps, may ſay ſomething bitter. Indeed, every one is afraid of him; I tremble at the ſight of him. I am afraid he knows the curſed ſecret of the mill; the only thing, however, in my favor, is, that no one believes what he writes or ſays, becauſe it is known that he will do any thing to gratify his malignity, or to put money in his pocket, as he is poor. I deteſt him, and I am afraid he reads it in my eyes. Burn all the papers in the little black box; we do not know what may happen; let us put as little in the power of fortune as poſſible. I cannot tell you the half of what I want to ſay. You ſee the troubles of my mind. O dear ambition! what do we ſuffer on your account! My hand can't hold the pen. Send me good news, for if my health ſhould fail, my charms will fail along with it, and then what will become of your dear daughter.

———————————

THUS far the original papers of the Counteſs of Lichtenau, which were found in an eſcrutore in the yellow room of the palace at Charlottenberg, after her arreſtation. The Author then proceeds to a narrative of the events whcih took place after the demife of the K—g.

Two days previous to the K—g's death, the Countefs afked the Phyfician, if the cafe was really dangerous, and how long the K—g might yet hold out. Four and twenty hours, at fartheft, was the reply. The Countefs immediately collected her papers, and had actually refolved to fet off the next morning. But the K—g's illnefs gained faft upon him; towards morning he expired, after a hard ftruggle, and the Countefs was arrefted by order of his fucceffor, in the Marble-palace at Potfdam. The red Morocco pocketbook, a diamond of immenfe value, both of which belonged to the K——g, together with a royal fignet, forged, were found in her poffeffion. She had about her, in hard cafh, 800,000 dollars, and the K—g's private ftrong box was found exhaufted. A favourite of the Countefs, a French emigrant, who was conftantly in her company, and then refident at the Marble-Palace, was feized at the fame time. Some papers, of a ferious nature, were found, likewife, in his poffeffion, and he was immediately conducted to the fortrefs of Magdeburg.

This artful woman is now in prifon. Several attempts have been made, by her affociates, to refcue her from her confinement, but they have all been fruftrated by the vigilance of the officers under whofe cuftody fhe is lodged. The enormity of her guilt is beyond all conception. She rofe from the meaneft extraction and poverty to rank and fortune; in the days of her fuccefs her pride knew no bounds, fo that fhe feemed to forget what fhe had been; many an honeft man, through her arts, was precipitated into ruin; and the ties of friendfhip, and the harmony of an illuftrious family, were loofened, and almoft diffolved. The new K—g, in taking this ftep, was not actuated by private hatred, nor perfonal intereft, nor yet mean revenge. To that Prince humanity, truth, honefty, and franknefs, will ever be dear. He has configned her to the law. The Countefs of Lichtenau, in the moft extenfive meaning of the word, is a ftate-criminal. As fuch, confinement for life probably will be her lot. There fhe may do penance for every act of injuftice and infamy, and the wrongs of the induftrious peafant, who worked hard to fupport her extravagance; there fhe may do penance for the millions of groans and curfes that have brought down vengeance from Heaven on her guilty head; for the tears of every helplefs orphan, whom fhe thruft from her door, but whofe fighs afcended to Him who punifhes and rewards according to the fcale of immutable juftice.

THE END.

www.ingramcontent.com/pod-product-compliance
Lightning Source LLC
Chambersburg PA
CBHW030007030726
47499CB00008B/2939